Swim, Duck, Swim!

Susan Lurie

Photographs by **Murray Head**

Feiwel and Friends

NEW YORK

For my father, Abraham Lurie,
who always knows when to dive in!
—S. L.

For Brody and Rosemarie.
—M. H.

A FEIWEL AND FRIENDS BOOK
An Imprint of Macmillan

SWIM, DUCK, SWIM! Text copyright © 2014 by Parachute Publishing, LLC.
Photographs copyright © 2014 by Murray Head. All rights reserved.
Printed in China by South China Printing Co. Ltd., Dongguan City, Guangdong Province.
For information, address Feiwel and Friends, 175 Fifth Avenue, New York, N.Y. 10010.

Feiwel and Friends books may be purchased for business or promotional use. For information
on bulk purchases, please contact the Macmillan Corporate and Premium Sales Department
at (800) 221-7945 x5442 or by e-mail at specialmarkets@macmillan.com.

Library of Congress Cataloging-in-Publication Data Available
ISBN: 978-1-250-04642-0

Book design by April Ward

Feiwel and Friends logo designed by Filomena Tuosto

First Edition: 2014

1 3 5 7 9 10 8 6 4 2

mackids.com

Author's Note

I fell in love with this little duck the moment I saw him in Murray Head's photograph. He looked determined and defiant, and I recognized that look. It said, "I know what you want me to do—and I'm not doing it." *I know what makes me look like that*, I thought, *but what about him?* It had to be serious. It had to be a matter of great importance.

And suddenly, I knew. It had to be what makes a duck a duck. This duck did not want to swim! And that is where the story starts.

Photographer's Note

Henry David Thoreau wrote, "It's not what you look at that matters, it's what you see." I apply this philosophy to my photography of the natural world. To "see" and photograph the beauty of nature, and discover the lessons it has to offer, has a few basic requirements: Take the time to know the subjects, focus only on them, be patient, and don't intrude. However, to discover the stories nature tells us . . . you have to see them with your imagination.

With Mama and Papa,

I watch the ducklings glide.

I do not want to learn to swim.

I curl up tight and hide.

Papa says a duck must swim, and Mama does agree.
"Swim?" I say, a-quacking. "Not for me!"

Sorry, but I cannot stay. I won't swim. You forget,

I told you once. I told you twice.

I don't like to get wet.

I look out at the water.
I want to swim, I think.

Floppy feet a-paddling.

"No! I'll sink!"

Mama knows I am afraid. From here, it seems so deep.

She tells me, "Take a closer look."

But I would rather sleep.

Papa says, "Please try. Dive in.
Today might be the day."

Ducklings say, a-wriggling, "Come and play!"

"You can swim,"
the big duck cheers.
"Take it slow and steady.

The water's calm
and you are brave.
Jump now. You are ready."

SPLASH!

"I'm in the pond! Look at me!
Hooray! I'm not afraid."

The ducklings say,
"Let's celebrate and
make a duck parade."

I dip my head, wet my beak.

The ducks quack,
"Look at him!"

Head to tail, a-floating!

I can swim!